THE SWORD OF JEAN LAFITTE

BY

KIRK MASHBURN

British Library Cataloguing-in-Publication Data
A catalogue record for this book is available from the
British Library

CONTENTS

THE SWORD OF JEAN LAFITTE

KIRK MASHBURN

My ACQUAINTANCE WITH Jean Lafitte, in the beginning, was of the most casual nature. In short, my household was one of a considerable number that maintained the prosperity of his really excellent grocery.

When, shortly after the removal of my residence to New Orleans, I discovered the name of the grocer with whom my wife had established trade, it impressed me as being singularly unsuited to his occupation. As a matter of fact, I thought it ridiculous that any commonplace career should appeal to one who bore the name, and who, my wife informed me, claimed descent of that olden Robin Hood of Barataria.

I am possessed of a romantic streak which even the exigencies of modern business have not been entirely able to overcome, and for some time this led me into the habit of personally settling my monthly account at Lafitte's.

I was not disappointed with Lafitte's personal appearance, for he proved to be a small, courtly-mannered individual, with excellently modeled head and features. A slightly swarthy complexion but served to set off his fine eyes to better advantage, although I observed a touch of pathos in their depths, and an expression of faintly bitter resignation, which I then could not account for. I had the explanation, some time afterward, when I accidentally discovered that the parish records vouchsafed descent to my grocer, not from the gallant Jean, but from his less appealing brother, Pierre Lafitte, and a mulatto mistress. Such lack of fastidiousness on the pirate's part promptly dispelled my fanciful interest in his progeny, and thereafter I substituted the use of the mails for the payment of my grocery bills, instead of presenting my checks in person.

More than a year passed, following the cessation of my periodic visits to his establishment, before I again (as I thought) came into contact with the grocer, under peculiar circumstances. I happened to be hunting ducks at the time, near the eastern reaches of Barataria Bay, and it struck me as a singular coincidence that I should find him in the same country where his picturesque ancestor once held sway.

I had become separated from the other members of my party, and the realization that I had hopelessly lost my bearings was gradually forced upon me. In attempting to retrace my steps toward the distant quarter in which I believed my companions to be, I was further confused to come upon a small bayou, which failed to impress me with any sense of familiarity.

While engaged in seeking a place where the heavy, sluggish water was shallow enough for me to wade across in my hip-boots without the necessity of a thorough wetting. I was relieved to observe the figure of what I took to be another hunter, upon the opposite side of the bayou.

I succeeded in crossing the stream without much difficulty, and hastened to accost the stranger – about whom there was something vaguely familiar. As I approached him, it suddenly dawned upon me that he was none other than that Jean Lafitte who sold me groceries. Simultaneously, I observed that his nondescript and yet picturesque attire would more appropriately have served that other Lafitte, who possibly stood upon the same ground when Barataria was a pirate stronghold.

A long, sleeveless cloak, curiously faded and weathered, and conveying an impression of impossible age, draped from his shoulders to below the tops of equally aged leather knee-boots. A broad-brimmed, lowcrowned hat, of apparently the same vintage as cloak and boots, drooped over the sallow face, where care appeared to have graven deeper lines than I remembered. I thought, for a moment, that the fellow seemed vexed as I hailed him. He hesitated for a perceptible instant, and then, slightly shrugging his shoulders, answered my greeting civilly enough, although without cordiality.

'I am certainly glad to see you, Lafitte,' I said, and observed that he gave a slight start as I pronounced the name, and regarded me with uncalled-for surprise.

'Indeed, *Monsieur*?' he questioned.

Lafitte spoke English with the curious inflection so often encountered in the southern parishes of Louisiana, even upon the tongues of some who are of a third or fourth generation of born Americans. He had never before addressed me as '*Monsieur*', however, and the use of the French title struck me as an affectation, possibly impelled by some conceit associated with his present surroundings. 'I surely am,' I affirmed. 'I've been floundering around in this confounded swamp all morning, and just about decided that I don't know where I am. I haven't even heard a gunshot for the last hour or more.'

'In which direction does *Monsieur* desire to proceed?' asked Lafitte.

'Back to that so-called railroad, at Le Boeuf station,' I informed him, conscious of a rising distaste for his continued use of the French mode of address.

'That is fortunate,' nodded Lafitte, 'for I am bound in the same general direction, and I shall be more than pleased to guide *Monsieur* to Le Boeuf.'

There it was again, and my rather childish irritation gave vent to expression as I reminded him, a trifle shortly.

'You've sold me enough groceries as *Mister* Stuart to be able to get along without all that '*Monsieur*' foolishness, haven't you, Lafitte?'

I was immediately ashamed of the outburst, for which there was little enough real reason, but consoled myself with the reflection that the damned nigger – even if he was almost white – was a bit too fond of histrionics.

None the less, my rebuke produced a dangerous gleam in Lafitte's deep eyes, and he stiffened ominously. The appearance of swiftly mounting wrath gave way, however, to an almost immediate expression of quizzical surprise, and what appeared to be sudden and amused comprehension. I confess to a distinct relief at seeing the blaze die out of those brilliant eyes, for the momentary flash, brief as it was, had given me a glimpse of something potentially dangerous in their depths. I repeat, therefore, that I experienced a relief even disproportionate to the incident when Lafitte lifted his shoulders in their habitual gesture and smiled, amusedly – a little contemptuously, I have since believed.

'So,' he queried, 'you buy groceries from one Jean Lafitte, in New Orleans, and because you consider him a very commonplace person, object that I – he – finds it natural, so close to Barataria Bay, to speak in the fashion of that – that *other* – Jean Lafitte?'

I answered him with his own trick, by shrugging my

shoulders, whereat he faintly smiled again, and nodded.

'Please pardon my unwitting offense, Mr Stuart. One will surely be safe in asserting that Jean Lafitte – the grocer – highly values your good will.'

I was strongly suspicious that the rascal found something in his last statement to furnish him secret amusement; but I could not be sure, so offered no comment beyond a noncommittal grunt.

The fact was that Lafitte impressed me in a curious and vaguely disquieting manner. I was at a loss to account for the indefinable antipathy his presence inspired in me; for even in Barataria, and despite what I then considered his theatrical manner, I refused to regard him as other than a moderately prosperous grocer – and a not-quite-white grocer, at that.

We trudged on in silence for a while, Lafitte setting a course almost at right angles to the direction I had been following. Finally, partly as a relief to the monotonous lack of conversation, which my guide seemed indifferently disposed to remedy, and partly to shake off the unreasonable disquiet which I experienced in his proximity, I hazarded a remark.

'I did not know you were in the habit of taking holidays in the Barataria country, Lafitte,' I said.

'Nor am I,' was his grave reply. 'I have not had a holiday, in Barataria or elsewhere, in more years than you would be likely to credit, should I tell you just how many.'

'Does one flounder through these swamps on business, then?' I asked, with a short laugh. At the same time, I noticed a fact that had previously escaped my definite attention: in addition to his queer attire, neither was Lafitte armed for hunting, as well as I was able to determine.

'More men have sought these swamps with serious intent than have come for pleasure,' moodily answered Lafitte, breaking the thread of my thoughts. There was another flash of that latent ferocity I had previously noted as he added, 'Some few have come to bide here the hour of vengeance!'

I made no comment; nor did Lafitte seem to expect any. I could make neither heads nor tails of his erratic talk, and, what with the wild and positively uncanny expression that frequently replaced the air of calm melancholy I had grown to associate with him, I began to entertain an uneasy suspicion that the fellow might be more or less unbalanced mentally – although the idea was certainly discounted by what I knew of him.

At about this time, however, I was further perplexed to observe that, although we were almost constantly on boggy ground, and frequently wading in mud or shallow water, Lafitte's boots and long cloak were utterly free of any stain in witness of the fact. The full shock of this phenomenon did not strike me until I afterward recalled it, in the light of later events. My attention was diverted, at the moment, by the appearance of the Mississippi River levee, which confronted us as we broke through a concealing patch of tall sugar-cane.

The wretched little railroad track ran almost in the shadow of the levee, and Lafitte informed me that Le Boeuf station was only about two miles above us, around the bend of the river. He suggested that I might see for myself from the embankment, and as its summit furnished an easy and natural highway to my destination, we made the ascent.

Sure enough, I discerned the settlement at no great distance up the river.

At this juncture, Lafitte called my attention to a vessel that was rounding a lower bend of the great river which rolled majestically below us, and forging slowly upstream in our direction. His face retained a mask of impassivity, but his eyes were like glowing coals, alive with suppressed but exultant excitement.

Examining the craft, which was smaller than the usual ships of commerce, and yet had one funnel more than is customary, I remarked to Lafitte that she seemed to be some sort of small warship. This fact, in itself, afforded me no clue to the reason of his interest, but he nodded an eager affirmative.

'Ah!' he exclaimed; 'a warship, indeed! And does *Monsieur* observe the flag she flaunts?'

'Why yes,' I acknowledged, after a moment's further gazing, 'it is the Mexican flag; and, as we are expecting her arrival for general overhauling in the dry dock of my company at Algiers, I assume her to be the gunboat *Tampico*.'

'It *is* the *Tampico*,' agreed Lafitte. It did not occur to me to ask how he came to be so assured of this fact, since I happened to know that the gunboat carried no nameplate – and even if it had, he could not possibly have made it out at that distance. Instead, I remarked as an afterthought:

'It is quite possible that I shall go with her when she returns to Mexico, if the authorities will permit it. Her commander is an old friend of mine, and he has several times asked me to make a voyage with him. As I have to go to Vera Cruz, anyway, to inspect another gunboat before placing a bid to repair it also, I may take advantage of his offer at this time.'

To my great surprise, Lafitte vehemently shook his head, and urged, 'Do not follow your plan, *Monsieur* – you *must* not!'

Displeased at the receipt of such peremptory advice, I was upon the point of making a curt reply, but the fellow was so evidently in earnest that curiosity concerning his motive in objecting to a plan that did not in the least concern him, let me to question him.

'Pray, why not?' I demanded.

'Because,' slowly answered Lafitte, 'Captain Manuel de

Ruiz, your friend and the gunboat's commander, *is marked for the vengeance of Jean Lafitte!*'

I do not know what reply I made to this amazing statement, or whether I said anything at all, but I do know that my last doubt as to Lafitte's mental condition left me, then and there. Probably he understood my thought, which would make clear his reason for explaining to me as much as he did – although why *he* should care for my opinion is beyond me.

'*Monsieur*,' he began, 'they will tell you that Jean Lafitte – *the* Jean Lafitte – perished in Galveston; or at sea, under the guns of this or that man-of-war – some say an American, and some say an English vessel. But they are wrong! When an American warship bombarded Galveston, of which Lafitte was then governor, it is true that he was forced to flee the island. But he fled, *Monsieur*, not to sea, where every man's hand was against him, but to the mainland.

'The fugitive governor sought sanctuary in old Mexico, where he had many friends. But, alas! he had also many enemies, and treachery brought him full into the eager clutches of the chief of them all: one Don Manuel de Ruiz, the governor of Matamoras.'

Lafitte's face contracted with a spasm of fierce and somehow terrifying hate at the mention of the name, and he broke off his narrative to glare malevolently at the approaching gunboat.

'De Ruiz was not one to pass by the opportunity to settle an old grudge,' he continued, 'which was only the more bitter because unjust. His end was attained by the simple and expedient use of a firing squad, unattended by such superfluous trifles as formality or pretense of justice.'

'But where,' I interposed, 'is your authority for such statements? With proof, your story becomes an important contribution to history; but without such proof – and that of a very definite nature – it remains nothing more than another of many interesting tales about the same subject.'

'*Monsieur*,' replied Lafitte, with an enigmatic expression in his eyes, and contempt in his voice, 'I, *who know*, tell you what is the truth. Proof I have none; but I do not seek to write history, and I am little concerned with what fate history may assign to Jean Lafitte. What does concern me is the fact that, as the Mexican governor's ragged *soldados* riddled his body with an uneven volley, Lafitte cursed de Ruiz with his final breath, *and swore vengeance on him, and all who bore his name after him*! And, *Monsieur*, the last de Ruiz, the great-grandson and namesake of the murderer of Jean Lafitte, commands that teakettle, yonder.'

'At any rate,' I remarked a trifle maliciously, 'he does command it, so that Lafitte's curse can not have been entirely efficacious.'

15

'Ah!' snarled my fanciful grocer (I still thought of him in that light, and found the fact amusing), with an air of baffled rage. 'Yet, *Monsieur*, the original de Ruiz sickened and died of a malady that baffled his physicians, shortly after the 'execution' of his enemy. The Mexican had laughed at Lafitte's curse, but there were those who remembered and shuddered, and peons who crossed themselves with dread, when the governor shrieked the Baratarian's name in the last agony of death!'

There was a pause, while the speaker seemed to be reviewing a personal knowledge of the event he had just described, so detached and earnest was his expression. There was about him, also, an air of gloating over that knowledge; but, even so, I could not forbear another sly gibe at his story.

'Yet, his great-grandson prospers,' I remarked. 'He is still a young man, and he will be a power in Mexico, some day, if he lives.'

'If he lives,' significantly agreed Lafitte. He regarded me for a moment with a stony stare. 'Would you know why he lives – why, indeed, his family was not wiped out long before he was born? Then, *Monsieur*, I will tell you: it is because they buried the sword of Jean Lafitte with his great-grandfather!'

I think that I snorted outright at this statement, but Lafitte continued his remarkable narrative without seeming to notice.

'The superstition of the governor's wife, who had a carefully ignored strain of Indian blood in her veins, caused her to seek counsel of her old Indian nurse, and the old *ama* advised her mistress to do a strange thing. There is, or was, *Monsieur*, a belief among some of the native tribes of old Mexico, that if a warrior's weapons be buried with his slayer, the malignant spirit of the former would be bereft of much of its power to harm either the spirit of his foe, when death should claim him also, or those living ones beloved of that foe. . . .

'*Monsieur*, there is often wisdom in what is termed the superstition of ignorant savages! Since the death of that old de Ruiz, his descendents have struggled against something more than mere ill fortune, and they have never greatly prospered in the end – but, at least, they have survived, thanks to the 'superstition' of an old Indian woman.'

I was strongly tempted to laugh, but something checked the impulse. By now, I was firmly convinced that there was a very decided quirk in my grocer's mental make-up. His appearance and manner, as well as his extraordinary conversation, caused me to wonder if his present visit to the old haunts of his pirate ancestor had not, through an association of ideas, finally developed a previously obscure obsession, and caused him to confuse the identity, as well as the real or fancied wrongs, of that other Jean Lafitte with his own. I remember, also, that I found time to be amused that his vanity had caused him to ignore the fact that he had less to do with Jean Lafitte than with his brother, Pierre.

I decided to be on my way to Le Boeuf, and thanked my guide for his services. He courteously assured me of his pleasure at having been of some slight assistance, and then added a final admonition against my proposed trip aboard the *Tampico*.

'A revolution brews in Mexico, *Monsieur*,' he gravely informed me, 'and strange things often happen when the passions of men are set loose, like wolves, to harrass their fellows. The gates of hell have waited overlong for Jean Lafitte, and I have a premonition that his buried sword shall again see the light. Keep off de Ruiz's tinpot, *Monsieur!*'

I should certainly have answered him in short and impatient fashion, except that, with a final courtly bow, Lafitte turned and climbed swiftly down the levee, and vanished into the cane patch through which we had recently come.

I watched him go with a feeling strangely like relief, and vaguely noticed that the tall, close-growing cane stalks did not even waver to mark his passage. I thought nothing of that fact at the time, and, dismissing my late guide with a shrug, I turned toward Le Boeuf.

It was then mid-afternoon, and I found on arrival at the

settlement that my companions had not yet returned from the hunt. As I had eaten nothing since a very early breakfast, my first interest was to satisfy my hunger. Afterward, my mind was chiefly occupied with the attempt to invent some sort of excuse plausible enough to forestall, or at least diminish, the inevitable chaffing to which I should soon be subjected for losing myself – to say nothing of my failure to bag a single duck.

For this reason, I completely forgot my encounter with Lafitte, for the time being, and so made no mention of it to the rest of the party. When it later recurred to me, back home in New Orleans, I casually remarked to my wife that she need not be surprised to hear, at any time, that her grocer had been committed to a lunatic asylum. Naturally, this statement called for explanation, and when I had given it in complete detail, my better half regarded me with a quizzical air.

'You don't mean that all this happened three days ago?' she asked.

I nodded agreement, unsuspecting of the surprise in store for me.

'Then *you* had better be careful,' dryly commented my wife, 'because I happen to know that Lafitte was run down and rather severely injured by an automobile, *ten* days ago, and has been confined to his bed ever since!'

'Bunk!' I scoffed. 'He may have been hurt, but he was surely up and out last Saturday.'

'It's not bunk, and he wasn't up,' insisted my wife, 'because I went to the store Saturday afternoon to select some things personally, and Dr. Marvin was there at the same time. I heard one of the clerks ask him how long it would be before Lafitte would be able to get about, and the doctor told him that it would be ten days or two weeks. I shouldn't be at all surprised,' was her added and somewhat severe comment, 'if your duck-hunting party was like some of the fishing parties you and your precious friends go on.'

'Not a drop,' I hastily assured her, 'not a single drop!'

I was answered with an eloquent sniff, and I was aware that the subject was better dropped. While my wife is probably the finest woman in the world, and ordinarily reasonable, those of my readers who have been married for any length of time will at once understand my aversion to debate with her, along certain lines.

In the meantime, the *Tampico* had been put in our dry dock that very day, and I was so busily engaged in superintending the preparations for her speedy repairing that I again forgot my adventure in the Barataria swamps. Otherwise, I should have mentioned it to Captain de Ruiz sooner than I did. When we were about two-thirds finished with the job, however, we were quietly asked to work night and day, to get the ship finally conditioned, and de Ruiz confided to me that, although his government had succeeded in suppressing the news up to the moment, a revolution was actually under way in Mexico.

This at once recalled to my mind the warning Lafitte had given me, and I told de Ruiz the story. Although I dealt as humorously as possible with the matter of the supposed curse on the captain's family – and, for that matter, on the captain himself – he, to my great surprise, seemed to regard it as not altogether a joke.

'Why,' I remonstrated, seeing him suddenly so grave, 'surely you don't take serious stock in such rubbish?'

'There is a guarded story in my family similar to the one told you on the levee,' he quietly informed me. 'How do you account for your grocer's knowing of it? Then, too, what of the fact, attested by your own wife and your family physician, that your Lafitte was in bed with a broken leg, to say nothing of a few ribs, at the same time you were talking to someone you thought was he?'

'You have me there,' I confessed. 'I can't figure it out any more than you can, but you may be sure of one thing: there is some perfectly logical explanation. One other thing, also – that explanation is not that I was drunk, as my wife more than half suspected!'

'*Quien sabe?*' murmured de Ruiz, with a shrug.

'Who knows' what?' I demanded. 'Whether or not I was drunk?'

'No, no!' denied the captain, with a hearty chuckle in which I joined, although not quite so heartily.

'At any rate,' I nodded, 'I am going to Vera Cruz with you, if you will take me, and your consul general will grant the necessary permission.'

It happened that permission was readily granted me, and the upshot of it was that when the *Tampico* slipped down the river from New Orleans, I sailed aboard her.

Once we had passed the bar at the mouth of the Mississippi, we steamed away at full speed; for de Ruiz had urgent instructions to reach Vera Cruz with all possible dispatch. The first night out passed without incident, and I was beginning to enjoy the trip immensely. I do not hesitate to assert that, regardless of what may be said of their colleagues in the army, the commissioned personnel of Mexico's half-dozen gunboats is made up of men who, on the whole, are remarkably likable and intelligent. Had those on board the *Tampico* all been insufferable boors and hopeless morons, the captain's private stores contained the wherewithal, in unlimited quantity and variety, to make us all feel comfortably fraternal.

I confess (with the hope that this may never be read by my wife) to having taken some pains, on our second night out, to avoid belittling hospitality – in bottled form – by refusing it. We expected to raise Vera Cruz sometime the following day, with war and disaster in the immediate offing; so de Ruiz, his *teniente* and I sat in the captain's tiny *salón* until late, smoking and talking, with drinks at respectable intervals.

It may be that I drank too much – although I think not – or it may have been the sultry weather and the closeness of my stuffy little stateroom that caused me to dream as I did, when I finally turned in. At any rate, I dreamed: and rather remarkably.

It seemed that I saw a disorderly group of swarthy men, battering in the door of what I took to be a tomb, or burial crypt. I had the impression that they were Mexicans of the viler sort, and more or less intoxicated, judging from the manner in which they staggered about, and the inefficient way they handled the iron bars with which they finally forced the door.

I saw them drag out a moldy casket and batter it open. What they hoped to find, I could not guess; but when they shattered the coffin and exposed its contents, there appeared to be nothing but a heap of musty bones. But there was something else – one of the villains stooped and held up an object that I could not at first distinguish, but which I presently saw to be a rust-encrusted sword of antique pattern, such as one sees in the shops of dealers in such objects on the Rue Royal, in New Orleans. With evident disgust, the fellow flung the rusty weapon back upon the ground. Then my dream faded into nothingness.

It was hardly daylight when I was awakened by insistent rapping upon the door of my stateroom. When I finally dispelled the cobwebs from my sleepy brain, sufficiently to rise and open the door, my early caller proved to be Captain de Ruiz. I stared at him for a moment, still stupid with sleep, and then it dawned upon me that my friend appeared shaken and distressed, and I hastily bade him enter.

He slumped into a sitting position upon the side of my bunk, while I waited for the explanation of his unseasonal visit. He seemed greatly to have regained his composure since I first opened the door, and hesitant to speak – ashamed, almost.

Then he told me, in exact detail, of a dream from which he had just awakened. And his dream, in every respect, was identical with my own! To be sure, this occasioned me some surprise, but the cause of the renewed agitation when I told him that we had dreamed in duplicate still did not occur to me.

'What's so exciting about it?' I wanted to know. 'It's curious, certainly, but I don't see any reason to be upset.'

'*La espada!*' cried de Ruiz.

'The sword?' I stupidly repeated. Then the light dawned. 'You mean—?'

'The sword of Jean Lafitte,' de Ruiz answered my unspoken question. 'It was my great-grandfather's tomb we saw. *He* has his sword – Lafitte, I mean.'

'Nonsense!' I sharply informed him – partly to cover up my own puzzlement. I was not so very sure, myself.

'I have not the matter-of-factness of you Americans, my friend. Besides, I have heard this tale of the sword of Jean Lafitte too many times from my old Indian nurse – that, and other things. I am absolutely convinced that drunken *revolucionistas* – or drunken *federalistas: quien sabe?* – unearthed the sword last night. Perhaps they thought to find treasure in the tomb. Perhaps—'

He permitted the sentence to remain unfinished; and, after a moody moment, smiled as if in self-ridicule, and lighted a cigarette. His composure seemed quite restored, and he still smiled as I good-naturedly chaffed him about his superstitions. It was still faintly in evidence as he left me, but I noticed that his face was dead-white.

Moodily, I proceeded to dress myself, after first ringing for an orderly to bring me a small cup of black coffee, in the hope of dispelling the weight which seemed to have settled upon my spirits. The coffee heartened me somewhat, and having no desire for further breakfast, I sought the deck to try if the early morning air would not additionally stimulate my mind to cheerful thoughts.

To my dismay, it had precisely the opposite effect. The sulking sun, hardly clear of the horizon, was a murky ball anything but provocative of cheerfulness. The air was still and sultry, and seemed even more depressing on the deck than in the close confines of my meager stateroom.

'I am glad we shall make Vera Cruz this afternoon,' confided Lieutenant Morales, the *Tampico's* second in command. 'I am afraid there is going to be some foul weather. I don't like the looks of things.'

'I don't like it, either,' I muttered; but whether I had reference to the weather, as Morales naturally understood, or to the uneasy and apparently unfounded forebodings that oppressed my mind, I hardly knew myself.

My own unrest, I gradually observed, seemed to be shared quite generally, although nobody else appeared conscious of the pervading air of gloom. I am afraid that most of the officers had imbibed a little too freely the night before – as, indeed, I may have also done – in a last merry fling before facing the serious duties awaiting them. Swollen heads and fuzzy palates would have accounted for their sourness, but nothing of the sort explained the sullen uneasiness with which the members of the crew went about their varied routine. The very atmosphere seemed surcharged with dismal prophecy.

Then, late in the forenoon, with our port but a few scant hours away, it happened.

Lieutenant Morales had just imparted the information that the captain had remained locked in his stateroom all morning, denying entrance to all save his orderly, who reported him to be drinking prodigiously – already hopelessly drunk, in fact. Hardly had the words been uttered, when de Ruiz gave them the lie, by himself appearing on deck. If he was drunk, I thought, he certainly carried his liquor well. There was a noticeable firmness to his step as he strode past where we stood, without appearing to notice us, and climbed the ladder to the bridge.

I noticed that his eyes were unnaturally bright, and Morales directed attention, wonderingly, to a detail even more remarkable, under the circumstances.

'*Porque la espada?*' he asked, of no one in particular.

I also wondered 'why the sword,' now that I observed it hanging at the captain's side. He was in fatique uniform, and just barely disheveled, and the glittering, ornamented weapon looked out of harmony with the rest of his ensemble, had it not been incongruous in the first place.

The nameless, half-formed dread which had oppressed me all morning now seemed stronger than ever, and I had a sudden conviction that my intuition was about to be justified.

'*Mira!*' ejaculated Morales, clutching my arm.

I looked as he bade, and beheld de Ruiz upon the bridge with his gleaming sword drawn, thrusting before him at the empty air. Followed the most remarkable exhibition of swordplay it has ever been my lot to witness. The captain's blade leaped in and out like a thing alive, glittering dully ominous in the grudging rays of the murky sun. Cut and thrust, thrust and parry. While the gaping crew looked on, de Ruiz handled his sword exactly as if it crossed another, held in the hand of a deadly opponent. Yet, the bridge was empty, save for him alone!

From where I watched, spellbound, the captain's pallor was easily discernible, and I could see, also, his clenched teeth, and the desperate set of his jaw. Drunk or sober, it was a deadly serious business to him, at any rate. He seemed to be getting a shade the worst of his imaginary encounter, for he slowly retreated to the bridge ladder, and having gained it, leaped swiftly down upon the deck, after a whirlwind of thrusting that might have been to give him the instant's respite necessary to accomplish the feat in safety.

Swiftly de Ruiz turned, and I distinctly heard his growl of cornered rage, as his sword again leaped up to ward and fend. He was strictly on the defensive, now, and gradually backed to the companion stairs. Inch by inch, step by step, he seemed forced relentlessly backward. Finally, with the same preliminary fury of thrusting that had marked his descent of the bridge ladder, the captain disappeared below.

Officers and crew surged forward to follow, but Morales awoke from the stupefaction into which he had been thrown with the rest of us, at seeing his commander fight an apparently desperate duel with thin air, and hastily posted a couple of marines at the head of the stairway to hold back the crew. Then he fairly leaped down the precarious flight of steps, I immediately behind him, and several officers close upon my heels. We rushed pellmell for the captain's *salón*, where we could hear de Ruiz moving about, swearing with low vehemence that ended, even as we ran, in a sudden, choked groan.

As the lieutenant gained the doorway of the *salón*, he stopped short; so that I almost bowled him over, so close was I behind him. I was taller than he, and could easily see over his shoulder – and what I saw caused me to gape quite as much as he probably was doing.

I have spoken of de Ruiz fighting an *imaginary* duel (and how else was I to describe it?), but I saw him now with head thrown back in agony, his pale face working horribly. With one hand, he strove to support himself against a table at his side; the other hand was clutched above his left breast. It was upon this other hand that my gaze was riveted with horror: for, as his knees buckled under his weight, and he crashed sideways upon the table, I saw that his fingers were red with the unmistakable stain of the blood that welled between them.

Upon the polished mahogany table against which de Ruiz fell was a small bottle, half filled with fiery, colorless tequila, which rocked precariously upon its bottom at the crash. Such is the complexity of the human mind that it takes remarkable cognizance of trifles associated with habit, even when focused upon other and far graver matters. Therefore, as Morales leaped to catch the captain as he slid from the table to the floor, I, quite involuntarily, rescued the half-bottle of tequila, to prevent it spilling and marring the beautiful surface of the table.

The ship's medical officer, who had been in the group at my heels, stepped in and helped Morales turn the captain on his back. His examination was very brief. He spoke to the lieutenant, and Morales sprang from his knees with his face sternly set.

'Someone,' he snapped at the wide-eyed officers grouped about the doorway, 'has taken advantage of circumstances to assassinate Captain de Ruiz in the interval before we followed him below. Señor Montalvo, have the kindness to immediately inform the guards at the companionway that none are to pass them until my further order, and bring me men to conduct a thorough search. In the meantime, the rest of you will patrol the corridor, and permit none to leave or enter. Go!'

Having literally spat out his orders, the lieutenant and the doctor took up the captain's body, and, between them, carried it in and laid it upon the bunk in the adjoining stateroom. With a vague feeling that I also should do something, and there being nothing better at hand, I walked over and picked up de Ruiz's sword from the floor.

As I stooped to recover it, I noticed a second sword, which had escaped attention because it had been thrown well under the table (or had rolled there). Curious, I retrieved the strange weapon, and then felt the hair prickle on the back of my neck. This sensation was not due to the significant stain upon the point, but wholly to something inherent in the sword itself. It was an ancient rapier, and very rusty; of a sort in use a hundred years and more ago.

Shakily I turned toward the door, impelled by I know not what, and saw (or, at least, I *thought* I saw) a shadowy figure in the passage, that made a mocking, significant gesture in my direction, ere it moved on in the direction of the stairway.

With the ancient sword in my hand, I leaped into the passage, bringing a sharp challenge from a guard at the far end. The corridor was absolutely empty, except for that one guard, and he, sauntering up, assured me when questioned that no one else had passed.

None the less, I felt that I had surely seen a face that I had seen before (I never could forget those eyes!), and I had had a fleeting impression of a wide, drooping hat above it, and of a shadowy form draped in a long, weathered, sleeveless cloak. These I remembered, also!

I *knew*, then, that the rotten sword in my hand was the same one I had seen in my dream – the same that poor de Ruiz had seen in *his* dream. The sword of Jean Lafitte!

I cast it through an open porthole, and put out my other hand to steady myself, for my knees felt suddenly and strangely weak. It was then I discovered that I had all along held tight to the tequila bottle. It was a small bottle, and only half full; but tequila is a terribly potent liquid. I didn't care: I was glad of it.

I drained the bottle, almost at a gulp.

www.ingramcontent.com/pod-product-compliance
Lightning Source LLC
Chambersburg PA
CBHW030535020726
47494CB00004B/1370